3%
HAPPIER

ANTHOLOGY CURATED BY

UTKARSHA ARVIND GANDHE

Inkfeathers Publishing
www.inkfeathers.com

3% Happier
Edited & Compiled by
Utkarsha Arvind Gandhe
Print Edition

First Published in India in 2022
Inkfeathers Publishing
New Delhi 110095

Copyright © Inkfeathers Publishing, 2022

ISBN 9789390882076

www.inkfeathers.com

*This piece of depth is dedicated to the happier days of the world,
filled with healing, care and magnificence.*

Disclaimer

The anthology '3% Happier' is a collection of 46 poems and 10 short stories written by 26 authors who belong to different parts of the world.

Unless otherwise indicated, all the names, characters, objects, businesses, places, events and incidents- whether physical/non-physical, real/unreal, tangible/ intangible in whatsoever description used in this book are either the product of the author's imagination or used in a fictitious manner. Any resemblance to actual persons, objects, entities, living or dead, or actual events is purely coincidental.

The stories and poems published in this book are solely owned by their respective authors and are in no way intended to hurt anyone's religious, political, spiritual, brand, personal or fanatic beliefs and/or faith, whatsoever. In case, any sort of plagiarism is detected in the stories and poems within this anthology or in case of any complaints or grievances or objections, neither the anthology editor nor the publisher is to be held responsible.

Featuring the writings of

Arvind Gandhe, Swanand Ayachit, Siddhi Patil, Savita Gandhe

Hemavathy N., Amruta Ashish, Misbah Iram, Vanshika Gupta

Harprit Arora, Santhosha V, Devang Dahad, Artemis

Rakshandha Nakshathram, Awani Mahajan, Nantra Nanjappa

Marshaniel Soumi D'Rozario, Mawi Suan Kim Shoute

Chandrakant Bhonsle, Anjali, Moreshwar Selukar

Neeraja Krishnaswami, Srishty Singh, Sonali Shirpurkar

Tabinda Tariq, Abhishek Sam, Utkarsha Gandhe

Contents

Stories

Meet the Editor

Utkarsha Gandhe, 16, longing for an openness towards conveyance, made her way through writing. Her realm of ecstasies, fantasies and real, raw love rules her extreme passion for writing, which in turn reflects through her masterpieces. She was 15 when she revealed her first-ever debut internationally, named Singing the Unsung, which is a biographical sort, standing out as a surprise gift of depth for her father. Faded Lights is here to gleam as another feather onto the crown and she believes that there can be no other harmony in this world than to be able to sigh around with mere ink droplets. She hopes to continue writing after her education and would be pleased to spend the rest of her life as a soulful writer. She has been a great seeker of The Emerald Tablets, and the one from circa, 3000 BC, impacts the way most of her life flows:

As above, So below,
As within, so without!

Editor's Note

This anthology aims at exploring the little things around us as well as the terrible happenings beyond that. It is an astounding journey of a million fervours of existence. May it be a little toy of your childhood or a broken but beautiful lover or may it be the challenges that make you stronger; this creation finds its way to heal you and soothe your soul with its lovely touch of depth.

When it comes to defining your life, there's no end to it. Each time you open up, you uncover it newly. And for me, this point in time was the cause that the book came into being. I felt that as long as you keep driving out the essence of being, all that it is tied up into is the 3 assets – past, present, and future, each one of them owing me beauties on their own. The past comes forth with beautiful memories and some life changing lessons. The future on its own comes with a lot of plans, desires, dreams and fascinates me a lot, and the present keeps me warm in itself, thinking of all this, bettering myself day by day and unleashing my own ways of living much more magnificently. This was a phase where everything in the universe felt like favoured me, and all that I came is with this piece of my heart in the form of 3% happier, spreading happiness, love, comebacks, healing, and a soothing touch to your soul.

My co-authors brought about even lovelier ideas to it, that I could feel the infinity of the idea, that life is what you choose it to be. These people added the true shimmer to this masterpiece and I'm grateful to them for this.

I hope along with the turning pages, you explore a whole blazing world of bliss, ecstasy, strength, and hope.

I wish you all nothing but happiness.

Happy Reading!
Thank You!
Utkarsha

Poems

Once, Always, and Forever

Arvind Gandhe

For once, always, and forever,
As rare as the four-leaf clover
A day of mine bloomed as a flower.
My soul was indulged into a happy shower
Whose ties had seized a so high tower.

One for once,
Another for always
And further for the forever
Each added to my
3 % happier.

My insight gleamed like that stream so clear
No house for dismay and fear,
With bringing over some sunshine days
An abode of some hopeful rays
A rooftop of some blissful stays
Into the mild oceans of soothing sways.

For once, always, and forever,
Rolled into layers of my
3% happier.

With my lovely souvenir
Much, much prettier,
A soul along the shadows of
Flare and glare.

My universe turned out as
3% happier.

Cherish the Uncertainties

Moreshwar Selukar

Wax and wane,
Statute of acts
May it be shadows
Or heavy showers of rain
You'd find yourself blooming through pain.

Down in the dumps or up in the rancor
The legacy would be seen fighting for the prior and the later,
Indulged in the work
Or willful at aim.
Perpetual attempts get better with the same
Everlasting efforts, love, passion, and flame,
It's all a destination game.
Setback and bounce back run on the same lane.

Plucking a golden virtue that you'd never thought would bloom
Let inner peace, bliss, and ecstasy boom,
The thing you would cherish
Exploring ways to your dream.
Hoping that your self-esteem won't perish,
Let the flaws and uncertainties gleam.

Feliz Navidad

Nantra Nanjappa

Onset of nights in perpetual thought
A wandering mind in its usual haunt,
An endless journey of confusion and doubt
About the thing I really want.

The time lane would have moved past us
You'd have deeply flown into me,
Why am I being unaware of my desires in thee?

A duo of souls so warmed together
Attempting to create a comforting weather
To make up a whole,
There are some broken pieces that I gather
But the ocean of time takes it either.

Thinking, rethinking,
Of why we restrained it for us,
When we could have either
Smashed each other.

Perhaps, the emotion shrank in pleasure,
Deprived in depths, we found it unbothered.

But possibly, moments stole the essence
Compelling to an unreal balance,
Concluding that it isn't even there.

Though the parts are omitted in me
I still wish I have nothing to share,
In turn, there's nothing to adhere.

Sometimes I wonder if you do the same
But it is so perished,
Oh, what a shame!

Though, I say, you relieved me of pain
You coerced me into another lane,
Why was I so unclear then?
Oh, let it,
I'm shining again!
I found a light,
That has such a bright flame.

What I need
And what I want from the world,
I'm numb to admit that it isn't you
From all that I have viewed through.

So, hey you, my blessing in disguise
Gone are the days when I'd get convinced,
I have something more to believe
You're a home where I no longer live,
Maybe, there my breaths blew
And my nostalgic sighs flew.

The flaw will still grip my heart
But I'll be above from these words of lust,
With an everlasting hopeful stay
Away from that so-called dismay,
A little happier from the very start.

There is Hope

Neeraja Krishnaswami

Yet like a pebble,
I'm still in the fable
Yet flew the vapours,
Droplets on the leaf
Oh, that morning dew.
Sleep pacifies our senses
Though, there begins a life.

As do lives hit a climax
Giving no hopes perhaps,
Yet we do hope.
Each one of one of us does cope up,
We hope:
For the good,
The better
And the best.

Ever and again,
It glimmers through an oubliette
At times,
Withering like the golden leaves
Hope stands out with it's so many hues.
Yes, we hope,
For, hope is us.
It sighs into our stardust
Hope is where our loved ones blend in,
Giving an astounding fragrance to the air
Where we are strong enough.
Looking for things to be fair
A flash strike of bliss,
Incomparable of any sparkle
Hopes dazzle and startle.
With wide open eyes
They wildly match the rhythm of us
Backing off to giving up,
We start stepping up
We hope.

Yet sometimes.
Hope ditches hope,
It beautifies the way we hope.

At times, when perception lacks
Till a moment that tears feel home,
Hope runs on its own tracks.

Yet it does
All through this,
Even through the waddled waters
Even through the dark pastures.
From every little piece of energy
Flowing through the deserted avenues,
Beep-beep, there's hope
Standing personified.
He is startling,
Saying,
"When there's nothing
You have me"

When there's nothing,
There's hope!

Happiness: Some More

Devang Dahad

Me, around the love that brims me
On the awakening rhythm that kills me,
The way my own starlight fills me
Until where, the bliss of mine reveals me?

Wandering at the grace
Delving into an ecstatic space,
Those pretty subtle smiles
And those talks from miles.

The rooftops residing beneath my footlights,
Hidden under my shadows.
Gleaming of the scars into moonlight,
The leaflets beneath the meadows.
Into the hope,
In the poetry and prose
My bliss tickled so very close.
Ever and again,

The dark side edges me
I scream at the cage,
To set me free
Stretching, struggling,
I invited miracles.
In a way, moulding
Rather than breaking the obstacles,
I rushed out to revive me.
Sometimes, the melody would heal me,
I'll sometimes be filled with thee.
Oh, my lord
My happiness is happy to see,
Brimmed with hopes.
Though, I feel a bit bothered with slopes
The way I tied my blissful ropes,
The happier, the more
The sigh, the shore.
Flowing like the waters in the rivers.
Me, on a journey,
In search of some more.

The Serene Happiness

Anjali

A flow of peaceful ripples in streams
Enclosed with a serene happiness,
A moment where
There's no wrong or right
Just everything on its embracing flight.
Melody of hearts falling in unison,
Magic hovering,
Beauty flattering,
Starlight showering,
And the aura sounded mesmerizing.
Blowing winds
And fragrant bushes –
Here comes my first light,
Here comes my fanciful flight,
Here comes me to me
And all the things alright!
Here comes each of the three,
A face, happier of me.

Blooming Out

Savita Gandhe

With the directions of the wind's flow
Through the fragrance of the flower row,
Through the gleam of moonlight's glow
Happiness is wherever I go.
It shelters into the pain, though
In my friend's love,
And that smile I had with my foe
There's always hope.
Isn't it so?
May the tide be high.
May it be low
Isn't the moment letting you grow?
Well, happiness is wherever I go,
Fascinating my soul in its flow
The surreal is blooming out for thou!

Nurturing the Rueful Heart

Marshaniel Soumi D' Rozario

Owing face to another day
Streaks of heartbreaks making their way,
You, my dear, I can feel these tears dry,
Though my heart yearns to cry.
Steps then retreat
Reality nowhere seen
Meeting the eye
But then I get up looking at the sky,
Embracing the day as if an eternal stay
My conscience then voices in a subtle echo
The show must go on, as they say.
Yet, my soul is so tired
Those so-called hypocrisies
And gobbling weary eyes,
Loved ones departing
And eternal dies.
How do I suppress this hell of a grief?
How do I now walk away

From these unending oceans of melancholy and dismay?
Wandering with an earnest heart
For a way to get them back
So, to speak, these words lack
Is all merely a misery to stack.
Though staying calm and a lot being still
Let no more nightmares cast their spells,
Let all the bad deals pass on and sail
With a hope that everything gets well.
Let those tears roll down your cheeks
Let it all flow whenever the thought sticks,
There's an end to every start
It's a part of growing apart.

Only if the time lane could have railed back
Into that world where all was fine.
That innocent, lovely childhood of mine
Where nothing is so dark that it haunts your mind.

Perhaps, these times won't fly to me again
But those memories would leave me in vain,
And all I learn is resilience through pain
Recollecting the fallen strength again.
For that dazzling dawn awaiting my way
For I learnt my love,
It will all be in you
As long as you stay
So why not a shining bright hopeful sunray?

Little Pleasures of Life

Marshaniel Soumi D' Rozario

Happiness awaits you
Knocking at the door,
Life would hit hard
You merely need to explore.
Contradicting emotions
They keep flipping,
Laughing, loving, waving, and weeping
Yet do the clocks run.
Yes, life slips
It is in the small things that it truly lives
Look for the bright side in bunches and hives,
Glare at the nuances
Appreciate your glances.
Tempest ripples, embedded in thy soul
Remorse and whine,
It isn't a foul
Nor is it an end to the world.

High be the head and euphony of voices,
Counting the blessings and silent the noises
Life's been merely a game of choices.
With smallest of the pleasures
To be sought the races,
There shines a peace on your
Loved one's faces.
Playing this saga of ups and downs
Paving a lovely way with smiles and frowns,
Ceaseless journeys of tumultuous emotions
Making it all with a bit of resilience.
Hardships, my lord,
They push to the better.
Bliss breaths in these ecstasies
Oh, my human,
You better remember.

Raindrops

Mawi Suan Kim Shoute

As I listen to the raindrops
Falling at my window,
Times flashback when I was
Stuck hard in limbo.
Never did I feel so down and low,
Barely living each day
Like a piece of domino.
Those were the moments
Of anguish and sorrow,
Winds of darkness and hatred
Swirling as tornado.
A whole blazing volcano
Making my legacy a whole personal inferno,
But, just as the fiery lava melted down my broken pieces
A happier me was moulded through.
Shining bright from smokes and ashes
Lord, the radiance glowed,
The light called You

Showered on me.

What a rain it was

That seamlessly flowed,

Just so that this heart could grow

The pores and wounds under the beauty of Thou.

The fear of nothingness that trapped my soul

Into a void

And that deep dark place

With your love that

Feels like raindrops

Raindrops on my window,

I found a glimmer

To let it go.

My dark grey skies

Flared as rainbow

With your love,

That flows like water

I rise from the ashes

For a happier tomorrow.

She

Amruta Ashish

She was nowhere,
Though looking here and there
She was found to be nowhere.
In the pages of the old diary
And in that college ID
In the wooden almirah and
The trunk given by granny
She was nowhere.
Though pronounced as Goddess
She was worshipped nowhere,
Housewife, then ignorant
Employed, then arrogant
This and that.
Bearing the whole world
Though she conquered battlefields,
Though she stepped on planets as Mars
Though she was the kindest soul,

Who could even design a palace or a dome
Always was she a cook on her way back home.
But then, where was she?
The real one of her
She was just a figure that resembled her,
Always occupied with taking care
And sadly, she was nowhere.
Perhaps, she was confined
To some corner of the kitchen,
Under the roofs of duties
Tied with expectations.
Fallen under bullying
She also had a passion,
A heart full of desires
Vanished in the time somewhere.
And then she wasn't her
Neither was she anywhere.
Though, there was a glimmer
Her existence has a shimmer,
She was herself there
There she was a mother,
Creator of a life
Something only, she could dare.
She is a zeal there
A new hope,
Origin of somebody
She is complete here,
The true one to swear.

To the More of Me

Utkarsha Gandhe

Coining pieces of regrets and shame,

Shot in a game of blame

Somewhere I forgot, there was more in the frame.

It was to the more of me

That bliss in the darkness be,

There was hope in broken to see

To my more, it is to thee.

It is to the more of me

Those explorations and hardships be,

Let your self grow and flee

Let it flow and be so free.

Hey, you, the more of me,

Give this to the more of thee.

Process

Utkarsha Gandhe

Waving, wading
Climbing and growing,
Rising with
Some tequila and blowing.
Awaiting the imprints for showing
Tempest, in storms and seas,
It is where my strength flees
Sailing through, to the wonders that please.
Together it all,
Recollecting the
Process!

Three Cheers

Utkarsha Gandhe

Hey, let's get out from the lies and fears
Console a moment for some three cheers,
Let's unleash darkness
That your soul wears.
Let go off the moments when you own self disappears
One for the past,
One for the now
Another for tomorrow.
Here are the cheers,
The three cheers
Of skies, depth, and many layers.

Nostalgically Beautiful

Utkarsha Gandhe

Memory, the word may sound a bit dreary
Causing ache to somebody's heart,
Tearing somebody's soul apart
But a soothing sigh falls over that.
The cream puff of the vendor,
The cinema curtains of splendour
Those oily hairs and shattered ties,
That *kulfi-wala* (ice-cream seller) going past my balcony
And the night lamps giving aura of harmony.
A moonlight walk hand in hand
Down the lane,
Together through soul
Nurturing the pain.
Each of the moments coined withheld

Lifting me up,
When I derailed
As of an ecstasy I'd have spelled.
A blissful shower and
The Johnson's baby foam,
Those tricycles to roam.
That bubble water with the oil
Those balls made of the silver foil,
And the names printed on the corner tile
Touching my soul from a thousand mile.

Pen, Paper, and the Writer

Utkarsha Gandhe

Under the roof of cosmic wonder
I explored a life 3% happier,
A perfect trio full of splendour
A bit of ink, moonlight, and render.
Pen, paper, and the writer
A way that can have barely a better,
Enough for a soul to flatter.
World is flat on a page
Feelings get rid of their cage,
When these wonders are together
Hey, the pen, paper, and the writer.

We are at the End of the World

Abhishek Sam

We are at the end of the world,
Yet do we begin everyday
At the sink, where the day begins.
The sink with its stains
And the mould on its frames,
That you've memorised so well
Over these stained mouldy days.
To that point, when you don't remember the sink as well
You've become a hardly wound roll of lacy ribbon who has
forgotten how to unveil.
Though you used to roll out
Your body like a red carpet,
For God to flaunt the flaws
You've forgotten things.
And you've forgotten how to remember them
You've used up all the toothpaste,
And the sink is now overflowing with it

And there's just toothpaste all along.

A mess of menthol, fluoride, and anxiety

Sometimes sounding seriously witty,

But it's okay

You've forgotten to brush your teeth.

Nobody does as well

At the end we fell,

Yesterday you felt you were at the end of the world

Though you woke up today,

To watch the colours of skies drain

In nobody's tomorrow.

You're on a swing five feet apart from your friend

With a red apple in your hand,

Crushing molars inside your amnesiac mouth

And you breathe and you sit, and you breathe.

And suddenly, you remember your crumbling crayon hands

Drawing a giant wide smiling sun in the sky,

Nearly two decades ago

And you remember you've began every day.

Warming you, watching over you

Reaching its strong citrus arms,

To tell you that you'll always remember the sun.

So, you swing with your friend

On red plastic swings

And hope you can do a 360 someday,

And you hope that 360 swinging revolution untangle your
apocalyptic spine

And help it mould itself into something stronger,

Something that can hold the red plastic swings

And two human bodies

And weight of the universe altogether.

But you don't have to

So, instead dwell in its beauty,

At the end of the world

Knowing that it has just begun.

A Bit Deeper

Arvind Gandhe

There was a voice in her breath
That had hushed down bitter,
There was a wild in her innocence
That had howled loud with the wolves.
There was a thirst in her eyes that had awaited the stardust
It was in her finest of the fantasies,
Where pain was a bit deeper
And a love scribbling over it further.
Perhaps, he/him and the enclosed pronouns…
Composed her,
A bit compact
A bit deeper!

Importance

Arvind Gandhe

The impact at the glance

The fancy of the flight,

And even at the edges

Hey, do you know there's something to confess?

Importance is greeting me with grace

It is asking for its space,

The dignity to race.

To convey the asset

Of the imprint of that sunset,

Of the dreaming light to let

A little fire to set.

A glimmer to take

Becoming so wide awake,

For that importance's sake

Eliminating the heck.

There's something to confess
Importance is greeting me with grace,
It is asking for its space
The dignity to race.
To convey the asset
Of the imprint of that sunset,
Of the gleam of that warmth to let
A little standard to set.
A hope to take,
Becoming so wide awake
For that imperative sake.

Hindrance of the Apparent

Arvind Gandhe

L- limited

I - Innings

F- for

E- expression

It's about a pretty separation

What feels good over,

What looks good

For, anytime, it can change its mood.

So shall yet in mind

Life may make a rewind,

You may find a stiff gut defined

Apart from appearance,

There's something divine

Some disruption to bring in line.

Let us cut off the weep and whine
The hindrance of the apparent
On the cloud at nine,
Let us make it alright and fine
For I hold the dignity to possess mine.
You hold the decency to match my rhyme
Let us take it to the end of time
Make the sorrows to sublime,
A literal fire and inning of the prime
With a little forgiveness to crime.

Wanderlust

Arvind Gandhe

The thirst as in my gleam
The wanderlust as in my dream,
Which embodies in the same
Dealing with the lame and blame.
Uncovering the shadows
Under the sigh of soothing meadows
Sacred purity of the goodwill of intentions,
The wanderlust opting out
From windmill of suggestions
A little with the vision of amusing animations.
The dark and the evil eliminations
I want the wanderlust to uphold the patience
And take into note my values of importance,
I want it to accept my emotions
A little we'd sway in its motions
Into those love filled oceans.

I want there to be some heart stations
Which would convey my intentions
And uplift the weight of hovering relations,
The one which would design my destinations
The thirst as in my gleam
The wanderlust as in my gleam.

Thesis of Purity

Arvind Gandhe

An equation of integrity
The brilliance in simplicity,
Thinking life can be pretty and witty
It's all about a thesis of purity.
Something to hold till eternity
A substantial solitude and serenity,
A playful interacting jollity
Hey, this is a thesis of purity.
With a great halt to compressibility,
Sometimes, full of unusual creativity.

The Broken Beauts

Savita Gandhe

Pieces and pieces
Shackled around,
Tired and lose to be bound
Whole, complete where cannot be found.
I've been among the broken beauts
Beauty is in their manner to pair,
Even through the great despair.
There forms an irony
Strange enough and funny,
More you break
The more beautiful you are.
Wondering seemingly
Infinite worlds,
Just like the moon
Proud of the scars.
I've been among the broken beauts,
I've been in love with my broken moods
And I love to be with these broken beauts.

Timeless

Savita Gandhe

Coin by coin
She would count on
Sound by sound,
She would echo it on
Step by step
She would travel it on.
One by one
She would number it on
Drop by drop,
She would fill it on
Breath by breath
She would kiss it on.
Moment by moment
She would unravel it on
But it was timeless!
The love-light dawn
Infinite enough
For her to feel on.

Yet

Savita Gandhe

Despite the storms
They faced,
They grew like rare flowers
Though the clouds
Came with rain,
They bloomed out
Like never before,
Though life came
With endless hurdles.
Their essence was the same
And they were entangled in their souls,
They were both
Together,
Yet!

Swimming

Savita Gandhe

It was a time
Of undaunted storms
And unexpected suns.
That's when the
Universe flooded,
And two strings
Embedded
A time when she
Drowned so deep.
It was when he
Taught her to swim
Swimming into his whiskeys,
Bubbling out with a rhythm
That made a perfect melody.

Faith Up

Vanshika Gupta

Butterflies dancing their hearts out
The cocoons just began their ride
What in the world is a tedious task
The ants have made their home at last.

A little bit of hurry
Leads me to worry
What if I'll never be good enough
For this mighty mirage?

In what dimension would I have it all paced?
Dropping my fuel engine in an empty space
What wonders would I have missed?
Disregarding all the blessings in disguise.

If my faith was just not enough
How much life would have flown in vain?
I can't afford to be this naïve
Breathing in such a hollow way.

Not being in line with fate is alright
But without faith, there's no way!

Positivi(tea)

Flt Lt Sonali Shirpurkar

One day I woke up to discover
My cup was filled with
Negativi(tea),
I had a sip
And it had an essence of weep.
Still, I gulped
And I didn't spill
As I stepped down the bed,
My slippers were slippery
I slipped and
I didn't hold.
I walked past to find
If it was still dark in the daytime
Or were my thoughts cluttered?
How was everything around
Seemingly so shattered?
I peeped through the window

It was so crowded,

And I felt so lonely

That I kept screaming.

Having no one who could hear

The smiling faces in a

Robotic style.

The warmth had vanished

And the depression had arrived

With my eyes closed,

I'm updating my

"Thoughts in Mind" (TIM) app:

Who am I?

What am I?

Where am I?

Oh, I'm not yet running the new version,

Am I?

Clicking on the

"Life is Beautiful"

My inner voice screamed,

"I always hear you beautiful!"

And smile at your milestones,

In a manual way too!

Open the (win)dow

Beyond the crowd,

There's a sea of opportunities to grow

The darkness of mind is in a hurry.

It is soon to go

The sun is shining

As bright as your ego,

The grip of your slip-pers is firm

Depends on the platform

You choose to run on.

Wake up and glance within

Your cup is filled with

Confidence, strength and positivi(tea),

Go get a sip

Break the barriers

And take a leap!

When Will I Reach that Frothy Beach?

Santhosha V

I'm on a road,
Deflated soul
Inflated ego.
I'm on the go
Excited to reach,
That Frothy Beach
Fearless of the salty sea
Bitterness will be fled.
On the shore, I tread
My brightened face
With enlightened steps,
Inflated will be my soul
I will not be on the go
And deflated will be my ego,
When will I see that
Frothy Beach?

I Sat in the Shade

Santhosha V

Sitting in the shade
Sunrays on the face,
Watching the time fade
Longing for something,
I sat in the shade.
Looking at time
And it had eyes,
Those eyes met me
And they seemed like mine.
Flashing so free
I blinked my wink
Drifting when I was about to sink,
I sat in the shade
Watching the sunlight fade
Gleaming an evening self-made.

Writing

Santhosha V

Shivering inside a cocoon of fear
Staring hopelessly at the distance to endure,
Mind is squeezing to get soul-stirring thoughts
Cursing the lack of words.
Tired of confronting
The demon of perfection
Loathing the self for not taking action
Lost in the journey,
With a buried destiny
Almost defeated
Coining up meekly.
But there smiled a saviour
Taking me out of desolation and fear.
Cuddling, I woke up again
I found hope in my pen,
Recollecting all my faith
I was now writing
Until my very last breath.

Membranes of Memories

Santhosha V

Membranes of Memories,
Truncated layers
Distorted images,
Deformed forms
Majority hooking,
Out resistance
A few though,
Uncovering insistence
Most of them,
Drying and dying
A few though,
Freshly sprouting.

Just One. Yes, One!

Santhosha V

I once got a chance to rise above the crowd
And I didn't see,
What others, too, couldn't.
I once got a chance
To raise my voice
And I didn't ask,
What others, too, couldn't.
Ever since then
I imagine,
What and all I would have seen
What and all I could have asked.
Ah!
I know, I missed
I know, I did!
All I need is one more chance
Just one. Yes, one!

A Thought of Thoughtless

Santhosha V

I was taught
To have my own thoughts
So, then, I thought of a thought,
"How about no thoughts at all?"
That's worth a thought, I thought!
But that's still a thought.
How did I ever not come to
The thought of the thoughtless?
I thought,
Is this really my thought?
I thought,
The one who taught me
Must have
Thought of this
Thought of a thoughtless.

Anyway, now that I thought

Of this thought,

See if you can have your own thoughts

I'm sure you'd have your thought of thoughtless,

Yes? I thought so!

Flayed Birds

Santhosha V

Flayed Birds
Tried to fly
Slain were the wings
Featherless,
They weighed less
Dried veins,
Beaks waned
Cared less to preen,
Prey in the sty
Grey was the sky,
Craving to fly
Before they die.

He's Not A Beggar

Santhosha V

Right in the middle of

Brawling Street

At first

I saw those oily feet,

Clad with frills of dirt and soot

Frightened face with a million threads.

Braced for nothing

And traced for none

Eyes he had, they were Alyssa,

A glimmer of will to live in him

He's not a beggar,

He's not a beggar!

Magic Shop

Misbah Iram

Escaping from reality
I wanted to disappear,
Hating myself
I sought consolation.
I discovered a treasure
In my wounded heart,
You were standing on the other side
Waiting for me to open the door.
I stepped in a place of comfort
Full of joy, free from worries
I made my way to you in despair
You heard me,
Believing my galaxy
You held my hands,
Through your melodies
You encouraged me,
Through your stories
Proffered me strength,

Inculcating your words
I'm no longer afraid to be myself,
Embracing all my flaws
Beautifying all my scars,
Taking me to a path of real beauty
Worldly satisfaction,
Seemingly captivating
Though you directed me,
To be the best of me
On a journey of choosing,
Betterment over perfection
I sought my solace in this
Magic Shop!

Happy and Hopeful Until I Met You!

Rakshandha Nakshathram

Happiness and hope
Fanciful a word,
They weren't in my dictionary
Until I met you,
Until that depth stroke.

Now it feels like
Putting on words
Like happiness and hope
In my world
On the pages,
Which were absent in my mind
Until I met you.

Yes, I'm now spellbound by words
In my happy and hopeful sum
Which was blank in my life
Until I met You.
Yes, I'm now connected to vibe happy and hopeful
A gratitude towards you,
Who made me happy and hopeful through.

Oh! My Mighty Mind!

Tabinda Tariq

Wandering around,
I feel bad to see
Why are you trapped in this cage?
Cage of your own thoughts,
Doing the things, you're not made for
Oh, my mind!
Explore the world
Live as if you're a free bird,
Break the restraints of depression
Uplift your soul from this desolation.
Oh, my gifted mind!
Let's learn to live in this traumatic world!

Ah! You're on Paranoia Trip!

Tabinda Tariq

Sometimes in life,

Nothing will seem right

Everything you will feel

Will seem as if a root cause of evil.

You are wrong,

You are lost,

You are lonely,

You don't know where to go.

In the desert of the unlimited possibility,

Paranoia will become your new reality,

And everything about you will seem like an illusion,

And it will be very difficult to get to the conclusion.

But what can thee do?

You are living in a delusion.

With lot of confusion.

But reality is that you are just standing in the corner of a lavish
party,

Just smile, everything is going inside your head smarty.

You are not on acid trip,

But you are on the Paranoia trip.

Feel and Smile

Tabinda Tariq

How soothing is the silence of the night
There are serene feelings everywhere
The sky is lit with thousands
Of stars,
It looks so fascinating.
Dazzling moon has a charm of its own
The glory when it is at its peak,
The night looks pretty from my rooftop
All the things that I wish to see
As I was waiting for the sunset,
The nature was in its own grace
Losing some things in the race,
The night makes up everything
When you are at peace and
Nothing disturbs you in the beauty of night!
Especially when you start to talk with thyself,
The tranquil sound heals a lot.

A Ray of Hope

Hemavathy N

She ran out of the house, gasping
Away from her parents,
Tried to find a place to hide,
Her ears fine-tuned to
Their footsteps' sounds,
The only way to know
If they are heading towards her or
She hid inside the surreptitious and dark space
Left under the stairs
She suppressed her sound,
Her ears wide open
Keenly focused on
The sound of threat,
"Threat?"
Yes, her parents fill her with
Anxiety rather than love,
Footsteps always give
Her the feel of eerie,

Every touch from humans
Was a reminder of
Those giants' hands,
Her hand was never held with care,
She was known as a cold person,
Beneath that label, all that she was
Is a scared soul and had a heart
That nobody knows except
Her pen and poems,
In the dark, she couldn't
Hear any footsteps for a while,
She felt a ray of peace
Aligning through her heart.
Someone was licking
Her hand behind,
A Ray of Hope
The cat of love.
Among the scary humans,
Animals kept her happy.

Guiding Light

Harprit Arora

Every soul felt pure to me,
The world seemed a beautiful place to live.

As the time flew, things changed
I was so broken, hurt by everyone
I felt so unloved
And carried no will to live,
Sooner I realised that it was nightmare.
Now, slowly I came into light and
Started doing everything in delight.
All I wanted is a happy life
Showered with love and health,
The dark hours taught me a lot
Ever for the first time,
I felt things falling at their place.
Some days were dark.
But the light was back.

The Way I Live It

Awani Mahajan

Living my life
The way I want,
Seeking something unique
Working for myself.
Not for an applause
For the life,
It should be expressed
And not lived to be impressed.
Cherishing every single day,
I'm being my own competition
Running in my own race.
I'll live my life the way I want
Perhaps, the people may not like it
They won't praise how I do it.

But it's me who is the ruler of the realm

And all I know is –

Live your purpose

Express the truth,

Share your love

Enjoy your dreams.

Dance to our rhythm

And live like there's no tomorrow,

This is the way I live it!

3% Happier

Artemis

Lost in thought once again
A familiar voice that won't stop talking,
The voice in my head
It keeps on speaking.
Demanding for it to be heard
Screaming louder when it's silenced,
That voice that no one can hear except me
Is the loudest that I've ever heard.
A little girl shy as ever
Who wouldn't share,
But always has something she wants to say
They knew she would change the world.
Perhaps, so
They silenced her voice when she whispered
But she was never brave enough to fight back,
She herself knew that one day she would be heard
And that day would be the day
She was more than just 3% happier.

Cry of the Wild

Chandrakant Bhonsle

A major assessment has confirmed one of our worst fears,
Global animal population has fallen by two-thirds in the last thirty
years,
Are the calls for wildlife conservation falling on deaf ears?
The animals are disappearing without anyone noticing their tears.

Human overconsumption seems to be the leading factor which
has been blamed,
And lack of action towards this adversity has also been named,
Intensive agriculture had played its part in nature being maimed,
Ecosystems both on land and water has been let down and
shamed.

Deforestation has gone on unchecked,
Almost 90% of wetlands we have failed to protect,
To say that we are eliminating wildlife cannot be truer and more correct,
We can no longer afford to ignore this subject.

There is still time before we are left with no choice but to mope,
We can take some concrete measures to arrest this slope,
For if there was ever someone capable of walking this tightrope,
It is us humans who can give our planet a brand new hope.

Stories

The Lost Light

Siddhi Patil

(Trigger Warning)

"Cause lately, I've been in the backseat to my own life, trying to take control, but I don't know how to." Every single word of the song was striking her eardrums. The clock had chosen to reside on 3. In the dark of the night, her eyes were spilling tears, rolling down her cheeks, as if it was the end of the world. She had just finished writing something in her diary, putting her eyes on the things she had around her. Finally-picking up her phone, she opened her camera. Staring at herself, she started sobbing even harder, filled with so much of hatred towards everything about herself, concentrating those dark circles, acnes, that nose, every single detail of her body, contradicting the beauty of her soul. The girl was screaming through the dark timelines of her life, not because had she lost somebody; by this time, she had lost herself.

Turning the calendar two years back into the story, Siya had been a multidimensional person, having aced several supercool assets, only to realise that perhaps, more the virtues, more the challenges.

Siya started feeling bad about the fate for her virtues because nobody used to like her. Little did she realise that in the lieu of jealous and narrow minded people, she was taking herself for granted.

At the worldly curtains, she was being constantly bullied for whatever she did, frequently becoming the recipient of fun and jokes in various peer groups. But, oh Majesty, you know, the same world on the other hand preached that fire burns from the inner self. Obviously, despite the little dark hours, the true self of hers was brimmed with tremendous and timeless golden pieces of strength. She stood, not letting herself quit on the things she loved. At times, it understandably made her feel worthless, but she didn't give up. With a capable and rock-solid heart, she pierced the glory of her virtues into her scars. She survived those storms.

But, perhaps, God was interested in extending the game. The storm, this time, was a greater one. After sailing through all the bullying, Siya soon realised that she was no longer the master of all, no matter how hard she tried. The bitter fact that rushing behind the world she had lost her inner beauty started draining her emotionally. Being good at everything, she had collected many coins of expectations from her people and also from herself. This expensive burden of expectations ended up being the reason that she pressurised herself for acing every vertical. It had been a hard pill to swallow for her. The way she was unable to meet the expectations of the society and herself scattered her completely. Her sandcastles were washed away, bringing clouds of hopelessness over herself. She was exhausted, surrounded by thoughts of giving up, harming herself and such travesties.

With such a deeply occupied mind came a night; the night with no hopes, lost light, when it seemed to be the end of her realm. She took the decision of quitting her life.

She took her diary and started scribbling. This turned out to be a note addressing her loved ones:

To all those who shower their unconditional love upon me,

All my life, I have always been good at everything since I took my first breath. I would barely fail at anything. Ever since my school days, nobody liked me, I seemed to be an uncool person to everybody. Apparently, I'm over-smart, I can't do a single thing properly and I just want to run behind multiple things. I'm ugly, short, have the worst dressing sense and what-not. But there was a fact that kept me going, that I used to be good at everything I did. But life hits unexpectedly. I have now lost all these proud possessions of mine and I'm no longer good at them. All I do is hush myself and keep doing that. I don't really see any reason for me to live this life any longer. Yeah, this was something I never thought of, but it's life. After all of this mess, I'm giving up on my life. And, by the time you all will have read this, I will not be here, though my soul and love would always be embodied into you all.

Goodbye forever!

Take Care!

Yours,

Siya

She put everything she had in her mind and just folded that note and slept, crying, sobbing so hard, tightly putting that note so close to her. She could no longer believe that it was the same girl, the one who was unique, dynamic, and magnificent. What a journey she had to travel.

The thoughts kept her awake all the night.

Another day came up. It dawned upon her, and she went to her best friend and in a really subtle way, just asked her, "What if I die tonight?"

The reply of her friend was heart touching.

She said, "I'd perhaps be living physically, but emotionally, I'd be dead. Because you my darling, you're my strongest support, my brightest hope."

Rightly they say that it is easy to love. But understand and accepting that you're loved hits different. Her words opened up the smothered soul of Siya. She released everything she was suffering through, and tears rolled down her cheeks. That one day with her best person made her realise that no matter how much of darkness life surrounds you with, you are always a source of hope to somebody else. So, start being that light for yourself first. It was a moment of revival of Siya into a completely different and decent person. Her apparently bullied personality now let her soul grow beautifully. Finally, she was happier than ever, living life to the fullest. With her virtues, the friendship she was gifted with and her mesmerising soul, she made it to 3% happier!

Always remember, you are God's child, and life is a gift with endless possibilities, which has to be unboxed by you before anyone else does. There's always much more of happiness awaiting in the backpack.

Wishing you happiness!

The Freakishly Capable Mind

Swanand Ayachit

Cedric faced situations in life that made him feel as if his frail mind's thinking ability was a curse. But he became aware of his subconscious and that it was aware of the positive and negative effects of whatever was on his mind. His mind played such a cunning game with him that it enabled his mind to be vulnerable until he chose to be selfish. He was actually playing with his mind, as if he had taken a brutal attitude to the outcome of his cognitive process.

His mind had its own way of keeping track of the information it wanted to remember. It was a wonderful thing to be able to observe anything objectively. It revealed his own mind's biases as well as a fantastic approach to manage his life the way he wanted it to be out there.

His thoughts, and the way he thought about them, were highly subjective. He never knew how much effort he put into performing the things he enjoyed the most. On the other hand, the same mind had the potential to make it greater than he ever anticipated.

So, always appreciate your ferocious, merciless, uncontrollable mind and put it to work by directing it in the right direction to get the most of whatever you're doing!

Painting My Windowpane

Srishty Singh

"The middle of an adventure seems like a nice place to begin."

A quote that I have lived, experienced, and felt throughout the twenty-five years of my long existence on planet earth. Circumventing obstacles, surviving, and thriving, perpetually on the outlook for the next breakthrough, time just flew by. Concepts of decompressing, regrouping, and reflecting on prior trial and tribulations are so out of my realm.

After all, there is so much to do in so little time; people shuffle in and out, experiences whiz past, and we merely spare it as a thought.

But who would have seen it coming? The inevitable Doomsday for mankind propelling destruction and devastation worldwide. As the rest of the planet hunkered down, so did it to escape the wrath of the pandemic of 2020. Suddenly, life was confined to the four empty walls of my 1-BHK with nothing but dark days ahead.

The empty streets and abandoned shops were indicative of the vacuum that sat in my heart. The adrenaline, the glitz of worldly pleasures, the excitement generated by external stimuli were amiss, and it felt as if I was deprived of every joy conceivable. Isolated with nothing but my own thoughts to keep me contented, I grappled with the situation. Vacillating between emotions from the bouts of unreasonable anger, downright despair to clinging on to hope. The immense time at my disposal made me contemplate a myriad of thoughts. What is my takeaway, you may ask?

Well, the unravelling of the events during the aftermath shed some light on how transient and outward our idea of happiness is. We spend eons chasing targets, creating a façade of mirth and merry on Instagram with gazillion pictures that we post, only to light a flame that is extinguished within moments. The skewed ideas of success and happiness that have been fed into our systems from the get-go have created a faux notion of fulfillment. As the world came to a screeching halt, your luxury car stood in the parking with nowhere to be driven and your retail therapy seemed futile as the clothes sat on the shelves. The hundreds of followers on Twitter and Facebook did not offer any consolation and solace, much to our dismay.

In today's day and age, where friends are virtual and love expressed via an emoji, we have lost ourselves to the vicious cycle of fabricating a life that seems to be picture perfect. The flex of immaterial things and forging connections online has swayed us and made us believe that 'this' is the new reality. We have lost ourselves in the glamour and incessant vanity of the farce. Under false impressions, that happiness can only be unlocked once you bag that prestigious job at the organisation of repute, or investing in posh accommodations, till you have forgotten to appreciate the little things in life that spark joy. The rush to reach the destination in this dog-eat-dog world has stolen the allure of the journey. More importantly, as individuals who work hard to sustain and maintain some necessary but other outlandish lifestyles, we took for granted the person who should be treated with the utmost care and love – ourselves.

'Happiness is what comes from deep within'; a concept that we all know on paper and in theory but fail to implement in our everyday lives. So, learn to nurture and love yourself, give the nourishment and food to the soul that aid and rejuvenate you. Take time out from your busy schedule to engage in activities that bring you bountiful joy, be it curling up with a good book and a cup of coffee, writing at midnight, dancing in front of the mirror, or decluttering. Work on the most important relationship that you will ever forge – the one with yourself. Make a conscious choice to disconnect and detox. Watch the sunset and bask in its glory instead of capturing it on your phone. Walk barefoot on lush green grass as you listen to your favourite track wafting from the headphones. In other words, everything that you are trailing is within you, deeply seated, waiting to be uncovered.

On Cloud Nine

Harprit Arora

On a pleasant Sunday Morning, having done my breakfast and lunch, I went to have ice-cream with my two little kids. After getting back home, we all took a nap.

It was 5 o'clock in the evening and my husband would generally be back home from work by this time. But that day, he was late. I spent some time with my kids and then made them go to bed after their dinner.

He still wasn't back home. It started making me feel upset. I tried calling him but couldn't reach him.

Just after a few minutes, the doorbell rang. Much to my astonishment, it was my husband's friend at door. It was a situation of psychological trauma when he told me that my husband had met with a dreadful accident. I was stumped and I felt the ground slipping under my feet.

I took my kids to the hospital, carrying bricks of strength. When I reached there and saw my husband, I was devasted. He was suffering terribly, and I was bowled over to see him like this. He was blood soaked and his left side body was impaired from head to toe.

He was in the ICU with lost memory for a complete month. He couldn't recognise anyone in the family. He called me the nurse and his own parents as Uncle and Aunt. My in-laws were gravely traumatised.

His collar bone was broken, left ear was bleeding, and a toe of his left leg was fractured. He was fully on bed rest with a restless mind. He would wake up in the middle of the night, move out of his bedroom, and we had to catch him repeatedly. He was infected after some days and had to be operated immediately.

Even so, the devotion, dedication and blessings of the family energised him to recover.

After a month, by God's grace, his memory returned, and he could recognise all of us. He grew so thin that many of his friends couldn't even recognise him. The revival of his memory was a golden & jubilant moment in our lives.

It was a new dawn for my loving husband & I felt 3% happier when I was at my lowest.

Mirror

Abhishek Sam

Five minutes ago, I looked at myself in the mirror.

I never look at myself in the mirror. It brings the same number of intense thoughts to the mind when one ventures into introspection. I tilt my face downwards when I brush my teeth, look at the old porcelain sink and memorize the location of the old stains in the bowl. I comb my hair without the aid of the cupboard mirror. Wearing a tie alone isn't too hard for me either.

Sometimes, I accidentally glimpse into the mirror and see this ugly, hairy face before I instinctively turn back. Facial hair covering my face entirely; wild, untamed. I never bothered to shave, because then I'd have to look in the mirror. And I can't do that.

In the time that I hadn't looked at myself, I was growing. Slowly, but certainly. From the weak, incapacitated cripple I was, I could see myself moving forward, turning into someone new. Although the scars of what happened last December still haven't healed, I am not ashamed to hide them anymore. Feeling responsible for the death of a friend is the worst feeling one can ever have. But I knew later on that there was nothing that could've been done about it at that point of time. Besides, he must be cheering for me from wherever he is.

The past two weeks have been a torrent of change in my life and my personality. My blood pressure levels have come back to 120-80 and I can walk, jog, and run. But more importantly, now I can live.

Five minutes ago, I looked at myself in the mirror. And I liked what I saw.

Stay Wild, Moonchild!

Harprit Arora

Becoming a mother is a heavenly experience. So was it for me when I conceived after 6 months of my happily married life. I knew my kid would find all the love and warmth in my family and I was pleased by all this. But suddenly, darkness surrounded me when I had a miscarriage. I was desolated and drained from inside. There was nobody who would understand my pain. Nor did I tell anybody because I didn't want to put stress on anyone by sharing my pain.

A year passed by, and God blessed me with motherly charm once again. We all felt happy and blessed. The first three months walked past us, and we were still filled with the same enthusiasm. We would dream of the loveliness a little child brings along home.

The waves of the new child always blur the pain of treatment. Doctors said that there would be no risk this time, and that gave us a sigh of relief and relaxation.

Again, after some 15 days, one morning, I felt a slight pain in my back. My mother-in-law suggested me to have a word with the gynaecologist.

The doctor asked me to have an urgent sonography and get the reports to her. I was in the most traumatic phase and didn't know what to do. I couldn't have endured another disappointment.

With my fingers crossed, I entered in for the sonography. I was constantly praying for my coming child.

The thing I had feared of happened. My child was no more. The heartbeats of the baby had stopped. I felt as if I was on a death bed didn't want to get out of it.

I thought as if God was punishing me for my unknown sins. I felt like I should stop existing at once. My abortion was scheduled the next morning.

I felt so sorry for the child who had to go back even before it saw the world. Some of the next days were heavy hearted for me.

All that I desired now was to see a child cuddling me with love.

After some 10-11 months, I was again blessed with pregnancy. This made me happy to no extent, but I was worried and grabbed by the past happenings. All I prayed for was that let this time make it.

The months were passing by, and we were full of mixed emotions. We were fascinated to welcome the child. On the other hand, we were haunted by our past experiences.

Passing all of it, finally the much awaited dawn had arrived. We were so much excited to hold the enchanting being in our hands.

I was in the O.T. As soon as the operation started, the baby turned, and the operation got cancelled.

The next morning, when the nurse checked me up, my oxygen level turned out to be low. I breathed artificial oxygen to be alive. We were all back in the state of worry. The doctors weren't sure of what would happen, and this disheartened all of us once again. We had lost all hopes.

Throughout all the ups and downs, dilemmas, and pressure, finally, God didn't give me dismay but blessed me this time. I gave birth to little angelic baby girl by the evening. And all I knew was the happiness and joy of finally finding the one I had been dying gravely for many times.

Tears of happiness rolled down our cheeks. The baby brought with it a glimmer of hope into our life full of darkness. And heart, it whispered looking at that gleaming face. You stay wild, my Moonchild!

The Loved Ones

Savita Gandhe

All my life, I have been a person who has had all the luxuries, money and what not. Everybody would feel a complexion by looking at my possessions. But it has been said that we know the worth of a thing when we don't have it. Perhaps, so was my case. I had money, but I was dying to look for happiness into people whom I can call mine. I was smothered of being alone, knowing that having a loved one by your side is a blessing in life.

What's the use of the dining table I've had at home if I have nobody to sit in front of me and have the meal together? What's the use so many rooms in my mansion when I'm the only one living here? What's the use of this great success, if I have nobody who would praise me? Can we certainly call this as success?

For me, happiness is in the struggle of life, accompanied by somebody you know would never leave you. It lies in a friend who makes pain look beautiful. It is in that meal mom cooked with love for you. Happiness is in having a loved one!

And I know I'm having a livelihood right now, not a life, though. I'm surviving, not living!

But I carry hope, that someday, I'll explore a life, finding my happiness, hopefully with a loved one besides me, for that's what bliss resides in!

Until the End of Time

Arvind Gandhe

Joey was a youngster who would always bring about interesting conversations whenever we would talk. He would talk about science, fiction, literature, psychology, environment and what-not. His mighty mind never failed to amaze me and mark an imprint.

I remember such an amazing incident with him when he called me one night. I was returning home after work.

"Hey, are you back home?" he asked.

I told him that I was on my way and would be reaching shortly and that he could also be there in sometime. His voice seemed a bit down. It wasn't the same Joey who would speak up with energy and enthusiasm. Something was eating his mind up and I was able to notice and feel that. I asked him about it, and he shared all of it with me. He was struggling a lot in his life. I felt bad for whatever he had to go through. Joey whined for some time, released all that was being heavy for him and burst into laughter all of a sudden. That seemed strange to me. He knew by my gesture that I hadn't gotten anything.

He started talking back with his grace in a lovely, mighty, and poetic manner. "I know that right now in my life, I'm facing a lot of struggles. But I also know that moment is going to pass. This certainly won't adversely affect the way I'm hurting at the moment. The pain is valid and incurable. But I embrace it, too, for I know that the next phase of my life is hopefully going to be better than this. And, it wouldn't be better, if it had not been for these tragedies in my life. Peaks and valleys beautify the journey. Nobody sees what turn there would be the next moment. All we can do is live our present, taking the essence of every single emotion, may it be joy or bliss. And then, just fake a big wide smile by believing that life goes on and so do we! I may not win all the time, but I'll fight, and I'll survive. My hope would breathe until the end of time."

Joey blew my mind by introducing me to a whole new perspective of looking at life with his unforgettable narratives of hope, which I would carry all my life!

The Unconditional Bond

Savita Gandhe

"The 3 Idiots" had always been the title Mishti, Sejal and Uma were called with. May it be a big function or an absolutely small classroom activity, you would always find the 3 together. Other students, teachers and their parents would always have an admiration towards the unconditional bond between them. But with increasing responsibilities, different paths, things started drifting their togetherness apart.

Now, they didn't talk everyday as they used to, nor did they have regular meets and share all the details of how their day had been. They lost all contact. All the three seemed to be engrossed into their own lives. The bond felt like it had disappeared somewhere with time. One of the three would feel that the other two had forgotten all the love they had within them, and so, nobody gave it a shot again.

Coincidentally, one day, Uma met Sejal in a supermarket. They were so grown up that they could barely recognise each other. And after staring at each other for a while, without a single thought, both of them burst into tears. Meeting a best friend after such a long lapse recalled a lot of memories in front of their eyes. All of them made both of them feel happier than ever. They video called Mishti and there was a gleam in the eyes of all the three which was soulfully signifying that the unconditional bond was still alive.

Getting back to connection made them 3% Happier!

The Gleaming Darksides

Arvind Gandhe

Ever since her childhood, Rumi had been an extraordinary girl. Varying from arts up to academics, she would do every single thing with efficiency. Having such a child made Rumi's parents feel blessed always.

With passing time, things didn't seem as adorable as we would have thought. Her blessings started becoming her burden. Rumi's perfection had now turned into an expectation. Her parents always saw her win. But as we say, there are ups and downs in everyone's life. One evening, sitting on a bench in a park, Rumi sighed for a while. Besides her was a group of friends, who were having fun games, lots of chit chat and a lovely bond of friendship, signifying unbeatable togetherness.

Flashing back into herself, little did she feel that she has always rushed to gain something, to make somebody feel proud. Fulfilling everybody's expectations, she failed meeting her own. In search of a secure future, she had always forgotten that her present was left insecure. She had been surviving in life, but never had she ever lived it. She always rushed for others, her parents, and their reputation. She realised that everybody expected a lot from her and with such dread in her mind, she felt like she could never afford to fail.

All these thoughts started exhausting her mentally; she saw no hopes. All she knew was that she had to perform no matter what, and that she didn't have the right to live the way she wanted. The fear of hurting her parents made her hold back every single time and no matter how she felt, she just struggled. But endurance has its limits. It was a dark time of her life and that one thing she had always been dreadful about happened. This time, she failed miserably!

And she had no guts to face anybody. But still she hoped that they would understand her. She went to her parents, told them about her failure and without a single of thought, her father started beating her black and blue, with a toxic thought of what the world would say in his mind. The person who was always with her when everything was nice, today, was against her when she needed him the most. This exhausted her even more.

Wandering around herself, all she found was darkness. She felt that nobody saw her efforts but focused on the results and became uncertain about her potential. A little failure resulted into a terrible judgement about her life, for all that her parents wanted was something to brag about. She didn't see anything out there which would bring peace to her chaos. She needed somebody to share all of it with, but she didn't have anybody.

She saw a blank diary and a pen on her work desk. It was 2 at midnight. She grabbed that diary and started scribbling something and just went on till her heart felt like. She closed that diary and hid it somewhere in the corner of the room. The storm had subsumed for her now. She had calmed down.

She had found something to have a company of and that made her deal with things better. Not much to our surprise, she was a passionate writer ever since that day. Now, she had something to rely on. The words would heal her like nothing else. She stopped berating herself, got back up and her next victory made a sound louder than her failure. This time, she was a winner, not for anyone else, but for herself. For she had found her calling in the world. She was living in a true way!

Everything she lost started building her back, this time, more gracefully!

She looked at life with a brand new hope and she was 3% happier than before.

She learnt to embrace her imperfections!

And, yes, even the gleaming dark sides.

Acknowledgements

I would like to offer my deepest gratitude to my whole team of 3% happier – My lovely co-authors for their support and cooperation. If it wouldn't have been for their encouragement, the anthology would have been just a dream.

Next, the biggest thanks to Inkfeathers Publishing for their amazing opportunity and enrichment to be able to compile this anthology of indeed divinity.

Warm hugs to my parents for their all-time upliftment.

Special thanks to my friends who patiently kept up with me throughout the journey.

Not that I shouldn't be grateful to myself, too, for the deep-down passion and love over this happening.

And last but the most wholehearted form of my gratitude goes to – Komal Joshi, who constantly helped me, checked up on me throughout the journey. She plays a great part in the success of this anthology.

All that I can do at the moment is because of the magic called words. How do I thank this wonder enough?

Meet the Co-Authors

Arvind Gandhe

Working in the field of educating minds for years, Arvind Gandhe inculcates the love for learning into children. He works as the principal in one of the reputed institutions and has been fond of the English language. Writing for the anthology of his own daughter made him feel happy as  never before. With the hope that the world would tackle the obstacles that hinder it from its destination, he makes his way through the book with his pieces of love and passion.

Swanand Ayachit

 Swanand Ayachit debuted as a ghostwriter and now works at an investment bank with a lot of energy, excitement, and a positive outlook on life. He has a really upbeat attitude towards life and is always eager to take things as they come. His writing is full of clear observations of minor details that he perceives. He admires people that work hard and care about others. His favourite people to follow are those who have achieved something in life via hard work, devotion, and perseverance.

Artemis

Just a young girl from Hubli, Karnataka, she goes by her pen name, Artemis. Her love for reading goes beyond her love for food. Artemis loves singing and vibing to music and occasionally writes songs. She simply cannot wait to dive into this little world she has created for herself with poetry, music and books and explore numerous opportunities.

Siddhi Patil

Siddhi is a student, entrepreneur and writer. This book is really special for her as this is her first ever anthology and this one, especially, is really close to her heart. Hoping that you all would enjoy reading this as much as she enjoyed writing it.

Hemavathy N.

Hemavathy N. is her original name and she prefers to be called Hema or Roze. Being a very bold and smart yet an introverted soul plenty of times, she turns out to be a soft girl and there lies a wild side beneath her. A 'modern melody' is something she terms herself as. She is into music and dance a bit for chilling. She loves to be admired and loves to do the same. She is the shade of moonlight, but you may also see the burning sun on the flipside of her. Breathing the air of the city of Chennai, Tamil Nadu, she pursues her post-graduation in Psychology. She is extremely fond of helping people. Delving into arts takes her to another world and her writings signify the type of a soul she has, deep like an ocean.

Savita Gandhe

Savita Gandhe, a soul full of passion and a deep outlook towards the world has made her career through English, and now, she spreads the same love she has for her subject to her students for years. Since childhood, she would scribble lovely pieces of poetry which reflected her soul throughout. She believes that life is a blessing, worth living to the fullest.

Amruta Ashish

Mrs. Amruta Ashish is the proud daughter of a soldier and wife of a banker. A lady with a beautiful heart and soul who puts a lot of emotions and experience into whatever she writes, she believes she has a strong relationship with written words. For Amruta, happiness means writing.

Misbah Iram

A 15-year-old empathetic and inquisitive teenager from Bangalore currently studying in 9th grade, Misbah is a usual daydreamer and a hopeless romantic, you can say. She's very much passionate about writing, speaking, open mics, psychology, and volunteering in non-profit organisations. She absolutely loves

participating in events and meeting new people and sharing her perspectives with them. She enjoys writing because it helps her spill out her unusual thoughts and imaginations.

Vanshika Gupta

A postgraduate in economics and a writer by feels, Vanshika hails from the UT of J&K, India. In order to find the calm to her storm, she started writing her heart out and so writing about everything that she felt at her core became her meditation. She feels that words have a great power to inspire and to heal and firmly believes in the idea of hoping against hope.

Harprit Arora

An inspirational speaker, author, soft skill trainer, corporate trainer and personality development coach, Harprit is on a mission to inspire 10 million people around the globe through her writing and public speaking. She has already inspired and touched thousands of lives. She wishes to demolish the three negative words i.e., impossible, depression and negativity from the Universe through her thoughts in writing.

Santhosha V

Coming from Bangalore, Santhosha travels and explores the rural part of India in his free time and reads in public libraries when he's not writing. He also listens to classical music and explores languages. Apart from being a writer, his goal is to learn Russian so that he can read the works of Fyodor Dostoevsky in original.

Devang Dahad

Having a deep insight into life, Devang, 17, loves to explore the different shades of existence. With a dream in his mind, he works wholeheartedly and believes in living his best life.

Rakshandha Nakshathram

Rakshandha's journey as a writer came into being when books of pressure pushed her into the dark room where she could hear her own voice aloud. She could shout out words in silence. Those words made her unleash deeper worlds. And, now she is here as a part of the anthology, carrying a journey from books of pressure up to books of pleasure!

Awani Mahajan

A young soul with spirit and enthusiasm, Awani loves to explore life freely and deeply. She is a patient and a calming human being who looks forward to achieving a lot on her journey. Writing poems makes her feel good and her thoughts mark an imprint on whoever reads her.

Marshaniel Soumi D'Rozario

Marshaniel Soumi D' Rozario is a passionate writer, teacher, and an explorer. She is a gold medallist from the University of Calcutta in Journalism and Mass Communication. She has been awarded and felicitated by the Calcutta Journalist Club, Public Relations Society of India, and Kolkata chapter (PRSI) for her merit in Journalism. She taught undergraduate and post-graduate students of Journalism and Mass Communication and wrote various health articles as a journalist for varied firms. This time, she has ventured into writing poetry for the first time and hopes to connect with the emotional chord of readers.

Anjali

Anjali, an author, has a deep passion for poetry and is always excited about writing articles. She enjoys reading blogs and writing her own content.

Mawi Suan Kim Shoute

Mawi Suan Kim Shoute is a budding writer from Manipur who grew up in New Delhi. Writing has been her most treasured hobby since she was eleven. To her, writing means diving into a world of endless imagination and creativity. It's her happy place where no judgement and fear prevail.

Chandrakant Bhonsle

Born in India, Chandrakant Bhonsle is a qualified lawyer and a writer, currently residing in the Netherlands. He is the author of the children's picture books "The World Belongs to Animals" and "The Extraordinary World of Cats". He has been awarded several accolades for his English writing skills from distinguished international institutions. He is an outdoor person who cares a lot about protecting animals and the environment as a whole. He believes that for the ecological sustainability of our planet, it is quintessential that animals are allowed to thrive in their natural environment.

Nantra Nanjappa

Writing poetry is the only thing in the world Nantra would do without any hesitation. "She loves to put her heart on the paper and reach the deeper worlds. It is in the hardships, that we find our courage and learn to fight," says Nantra.

Moreshwar Selukar

Moreshwar, a passionate poet, started writing poetry at the age of 13. He loves to write based on his observations about society, views towards it and understanding of the same. In his poems, he expresses a viewpoint of a middle-class boy. Majorly, his poems are based on books read by him, experiences of places visited and the nature of people around him. He writes in two languages, Marathi and English.

Neeraja Krishnaswami

Neeraja Krishnaswami is a post-graduate in Business Management, an Accounts Executive with her father, and a blogger by choice. Writing being her passion, she has participated in poetry and story writing competitions and is a co-author in anthologies. Apart from writing, her hobbies are singing, painting and landscape photography.

Srishty Singh

An engineer by trade, Srishty left her cushy tech job in the year 2020 to pursue her passion for writing. Treading down an unknown path was difficult nevertheless, but she kept the ember of intent burning. It has been a humbling and gratifying two years of weaving stories and there is no looking back, for the universe always falls in love with a stubborn heart.

Sonali Shirpurkar

Flight Lieutenant Sonali Shirpurkar (EX IAF Officer), known by many titles such as Mrs. India Adventurous, author, passionate emcee, personality development trainer motivational speaker, kathak dancer, and yoga instructor, served in the Indian Air Force as a Short Service  Commissioned Officer for 6 years in Aeronautical Engineering Stream. She is an Electrical Engineer with MBA in Information Technology and has done Business Administration from the Indian Institute of Management Calcutta (IIMC).

She does social work with a lot of passion and her kindness is the virtue that makes her soul even more graceful.

Tabinda Tariq

 Tabinda Tariq is a teenage girl hailing from Kashmir who wants everyone to heal their chaotic souls through her poetry. She feels the real essence of felicity while scribbling those thoughts and pure emotions that she feels around herself. Her poems have been published in several anthologies. She likes being able to make her writing something other people can connect to or relate to in some way by generalising the notions and experiences she is writing about. She believes more in spirituality. Moreover, she wants to lay down her

life for the noble cause of popularising the education of poetry and the writing and longs to serve humanity with sincerity.

Abhishek Sam

A Virgo thespian with a flair for the dramatic, Abhishek spends his time playing video games and writing scripts about people who love video games. Originally from Kerala, he settled down in Pune after graduating from Symbiosis School for Liberal Arts. Currently an editor at Zoopero  Marketing Ltd., Abhishek continues to foster his affinity for languages, accessibility, and education. He passes his time translating anime openings into his mother tongue, Malayalam, and singing them to his little sister.

INKFEATHERS PUBLISHING

India's Most Author Friendly Publishing House

Stay updated about the latest books, anthologies, events, exclusive offers, contests, product giveaways and other things that we do to support authors.

 Inkfeathers Publishing

 @InkfeathersPublishing

 @_Inkfeathers

 @Inkfeathers

 Inkfeathers.com

We'd love to connect with you!

www.ingramcontent.com/pod-product-compliance
Lightning Source LLC
Chambersburg PA
CBHW020529160726
47992CB00005BA/2305